# *what matters*

God bless you
love
*[signature]*

*Debra*
*Butler*

# *what*
# *matters*

the promise

## TATE PUBLISHING
AND ENTERPRISES, LLC

Published by Tate Publishing & Enterprises, LLC
127 E. Trade Center Terrace | Mustang, Oklahoma 73064 USA
1.888.361.9473 | www.tatepublishing.com

Tate Publishing is committed to excellence in the publishing industry. The company reflects the philosophy established by the founders, based on Psalm 68:11,
*"The Lord gave the word and great was the company of those who published it."*

Published in the United States of America

ISBN: 978-1-63185-061-5
Poetry / General
14.04.04

*This book is dedicated to God almighty maker of heaven and earth, of all that is seen and unseen.*

*I put my faith and hope in His strength and in His power and in His wisdom and in His never-ending love for me.*

This book continues to be a great gift to us all. And I continue to use the gift God has given me because I never want to lose it. It isn't simply the fact that God has enabled me to rhyme words (something He nurtured in me since childhood) but it's the awesome depth of meaning, the message that comes through, the teaching that I didn't have (at least not that I knew of) until after the poem was finished. I enjoyed a great Bible study with wonderful people where a question would be asked and I'd answer it and people around me would say "How did you know that?" and my response would be "I don't know". It's almost as if God gave me the ability to write along with certain knowledge that would be there when I called upon it to make the writings more meaningful with a lesson in them.

I love God; let's just get that out there. I am a true fan of His. I talk about Him all the time. I talk about Him to people who I can watch be lifted as we're talking and to people who become uncomfortable about the whole thing. One such friend told me he and his family believed in something else and I left it at that. A few days later he sat across the room from me and with his finger he invited me over and said "Tell me about your God". And I did and we had an in-depth conversation and the next day I presented him with a signed copy of "What Matters" with a personal note in it and he was visibly moved and has told me since that he reads it often.

In the past few years I have been so blessed to be able to watch what this book "What Matters" does to people. I gave a copy to a Pastor at a local church and after he read it we talked about it and about God in general and when we were done he told me that I was a living gospel. That was one of the nicest compliments I had ever received. I have heard from people who gave "What Matters" to people who called them crying almost invariably saying it was just what they needed. A woman had my book in her car when she went to see a sick friend just out of the hospital. She had forgotten the gift she got for her so she gave her my book instead. She said her friend called her crying and said "Many people came and brought me food but no one brought anything for my soul". A co-worker of mine had been sick and was very depressed and when I gave her my book she said "I feel I'm being lifted just holding this book". I gave the book to several of Brooke's close friends for their parents and find it so rewarding to be told that they have the book on their cocktail table or on their nightstand so they can read it before going to sleep. Believe me I do not go about handing out books to everyone I see or even to everyone I know. Something moves me to give it to them and it's always at a time when they need it most. Maybe there's never a time we don't need it. I sent a copy to a childhood friend in a Christmas card, not sure why, I just felt I should and I was taking a chance that she might think I was "out there" but later she told me how she had lost both her parents suddenly, tragically and that the book helped her so much. She has been an encouragement to me and my writing ever since then. God lets me know somehow when I should give someone a book or He just leads me to them.

One time I backed out of a parking space just as a woman was pulling out behind me and our cars kind of slid off each other's. We got out and she started telling me how she had her niece in the car and her sister was in the hospital and they were rushing around trying to get ready for Thanksgiving and they were going to the hospital so her niece could see her mother and she was very anxious. We took down each other's information and I started telling her how it was all going to work out and not to let it all get to her and then I realized that I had used my book to put the paper on so I could write. I then gave the book to her and told her again that everything would be all right and I went to work. She had my book and my contact numbers and a few hours later she called me and she was crying worse than she was when I left her and she was trying to tell me that she was reading my book and that the book was helping her so much that it was "just what she needed". I backed my car into her car and my family received Thanksgiving and Christmas cards from her thanking me for "What Matters". I asked God if He could bring them to me without actually having me run into their cars to get their attention.

Sometimes what God asks of us is more difficult than other times. I've learned you just need to stay in prayer and listen to nothing else but the voice of God. I was scared to death to do this thing but God would lead me to passages in the Bible where it says things like "I have laid kings and princes at your feet" and when I told God that I couldn't do it He spoke plainly to me and said I had to and I, almost defiantly said, "Then you have to give me the courage" and I turned on the TV and flipped through a few channels, got to the history channel just in time to watch David hurl the stone at Goliath and kill him. The announcer came on and said "They were held captive until someone with enough <u>courage</u> came along to free them". It was exactly the same word I had used a few moments earlier and I did feel courageous. But then I started listening to people instead of God and the fear became too great. Once that happened it was all over; I could no longer do what God had asked of me. That brought me to write "Fear Nothing But Fear Itself" because God was going to do great things for me for standing up for Him, He was bringing me to the "good land" but because of my fear, my lack of faith, I couldn't take that good land. Fear is our biggest enemy. It is the opposite of faith.

Not long after that I dropped my wallet twice in the span of a few weeks in two different grocery stores. The first time the store called to say they had it I raced to the store praying that my money, draped across the wallet, and the cards would still be there. The woman handed me my wallet, with the money still draped across it hanging out the sides and all the cards were there. The second time the store called I thought it had to be some kind of a mistake but they assured me they had my wallet. I got into my car started racing to the store again and started praying and said God I have no right to ask you this, I just did this, but please let my money (again draped across the wallet), and my cards be there. I walked in and again was handed my wallet exactly as it was the last time I had seen it. It hasn't happened since but I felt very strongly that God was telling me He had my back just as I had His when I called powerful people out. It made them see the truth and hate the sin which is what God wanted.

My relationship with God has always been very strong since I was a little girl. I would play in my yard by myself before I was old enough to go to school and I would talk to Jesus as if He was my friend playing with me out there just digging in the dirt, doing whatever. I always felt very close to Him. The first edition of "What Matters" is very personal, it's my personal relationship with God, me personally getting closer to Him. The poems included in the second edition were written later and they somehow seem to be more of a teaching nature. My mom is a huge fan of mine, always has been, and she tells me that I take Scripture and put it into words that you can apply to your everyday life. The truth is the Bible is timeless it is just as relevant today if not more so than it was when it was written. It is a treasure that most people don't realize they have. I am able to spend some time with my Bible every morning no matter what my schedule is. It is God's way of communicating with us. Everything that has happened, everything that is happening now and everything that will happen is written about in the Bible along with everything in between.

There are 37 miracles recorded in the Bible that were performed by Jesus. I find the most interesting to be the ones where Jesus casts demons out of people. The demons almost always address Jesus, they know Him because Jesus was there when God created the angels and they always ask Him things like "Son of God what do you want from us? Are you here to destroy us before the appointed time?" I love that. I love that they know He is without question the Son of God, and that He will destroy them at the chosen time. The Bible tells us that many were brought to Him on various occasions so that He could heal them and that every person who even touched His robe was healed. The number of miracles actually performed during this time are too numerous to be written down; the world could not hold the books that would be written. The Bible allows us to see Jesus as God and it allows people today to believe and be healed and saved. Jesus is still healing people and saving people who believe every day.

When I realized that I had been given a gift I told my husband Harry that since it was a gift from God I was going to use it for God's glory and I wrote "Your Love" which is the first poem in this book because it deserves to be so. I thank my husband, Harry, for going through it all with me. I remember taking the poem to work and letting some of the older tough men operating heavy excavating equipment read it and I watched them as they read it and saw that it had touched them and one of them told me it could be the new Amazing Grace. It is so simple but still one of my favorites, a prayer straight to God. There is so much truth in that poem and I have used it to help people. The line "My faith in your love I believe is what saved me, and the more my faith grew the more Satan craved me" has so much more meaning than I knew it had when I wrote it. The devil's sole purpose in this world is to get us away from believing in God and all that He can do for us and he hates whenever we get closer to God so when we do he attacks us even harder. I had a friend come to visit me and she told me she was praying, she was doing everything she was supposed to do and she was getting closer to God but bad things kept happening. I gave her a copy of "What Matters" and opened to "Your Love" and explained the line to her telling her that the devil wants to make her question her actions, he wants her to say what's the sense in doing all this, praying like this, it isn't helping anyway. I told her that she should rejoice because it's her sign that she's getting closer to God and so the devil is bringing all these obstacles to her to try to get her to stop believing. I asked her to just take the next step with courage and faith. And she did.

"The Promise" is one of my favorite poems but I wasn't aware of the depth of some of those words until later. "There He stood larger than life..." because He was at that time larger than life. Jesus came into the world by the word becoming flesh and then He was killed for our sakes and rose from death to another state we can't even fathom, which is definitely larger than life. And then "knowing how He had suffered right to the bitter end." I was given thoughts and words to rhyme but when I wrote these words I was not thinking about the bitter wine given to Jesus right before He died but that is what I wrote. Those are the words that were given to me to write. That is why I never want to lose this gift I've been given. It is such an amazing privilege to be able to have these words come through me as they do. I consider myself a small soldier is an awesomely large army. I am so grateful to be a part of this whole thing. God is truly awesome, protecting me every step of the way.

I put myself out there all the time preaching about how important faith is and that knowing you're blessed is the first step to being truly blessed. I say it's like a parent who does something good for a child and the child isn't that impressed and so they're reluctant to do something else. Then you have the child you do something good for who is so grateful and impressed by what you did that you can't wait to do something else for them. God makes awesome things happen for me and I tell people about the great things He does, in spite of the fact that some might think I'm nuts, so they can see the things He does and believe that faith can do that for them as well. And like the parent I feel God says, "Really you think that was good, watch what I can really do". And so you're continually blessed.

Expectation, the thoughts in our heads shape our lives. It is very true that when you expect good to happen, if you keep your thoughts on good things your life will be happy and it will be a good life. However, if you expect bad things to happen and keep your thoughts on the negative in your life, talk to everyone about your problems, your life will be consumed with what is wrong, the things you don't have, and because you're expecting more bad things to happen they will. "When it rains it pours". Who hasn't heard that? That's because you spend your time thinking about the one thing that went wrong and so you cause more things to go wrong making it impossible for you to be happy. Did you ever wake up with an ungrateful heart and complain about something and then something actually terrible happens? You find yourself saying I'm sorry God I didn't mean to complain please give me back the problems I had this morning they really weren't bad at all. And we've all heard "If you can see it you can be it". That's because everything first begins with a single thought, good or bad. Just as Jesus warned us that if we even think of sin we've already committed it because the thought brings it to be. So it makes sense that if we think about the good things we want to achieve, the good life we want to live, we will manifest that into our lives. And if we think that God will provide for us He will.

Faith. I don't think there's anything more important to possess in this world but faith. People are continually trying to kill faith, disprove the very existence of God. There are TV shows dedicated to disproving the Bible, that's all they do. I say Faith stands for Feeling As If That's Happened. That means when you pray for something feel like what you're praying for has already been granted and it will be. It means feeling in the depth of your soul that the words in the Bible, the stories in the Bible happened, without question, without investigation, just knowing. Faith is the first step to a relationship with God. No matter how much they try to disprove God, the fact is we are still concerned enough with Him to try to disprove Him, we are still talking about Him, reading about Him, praying to Him, and counting on Him to continue to love us and protect us. The woman following Jesus who had been hemorrhaging for years touched His robe feeling that if she could just touch it she could be healed. Jesus knew someone had been healed and turned to see who it was and told the woman that her faith had healed her. Feeling as if that's happened, before she even touched His robe she believed she would be healed. That's what faith can do.

Some people only talk to God when they find themselves in trouble and some people talk to Him all the time until they find themselves in trouble. We need God in the best times, to rejoice with Him and thank Him for the good in our lives and we need God when we fall short, which we all do, that doesn't mean you can no longer talk to Him. On the contrary that's when we need to talk to Him most. One of my darkest poems "The Edge" is about just that. When we do find ourselves at the end of our rope losing all hope that's when we must reach out to God because He will never forsake us, even in our darkest days. The devil loves when we fall short, he's right there telling you that you're no good anymore, that God doesn't want to hear from you that you have no right to go to Him. He separates us from God and thereby achieves his goal. It takes great faith to lift yourself from that but you can, we all can. That's the great message. No matter what, you can always go back to God and He will always take you back and be so happy to do so; He rejoices at our return.

We are all tempted by sin. Jesus was tempted throughout his entire ministry when He was in the desert up until the time of the cross when Satan wanted nothing more than to have Jesus walk away from the cross making any hope for our salvation impossible. The devil is very evil and he will use anything he can to cause us to sin. A strong lesson in the Second Edition comes from "Seven More". When we overcome sin we must cling to Jesus so that it does not enter us again. The Bible tells us that a demon was cast out of a man and he came back and found the house swept clean so he brought seven more demons back with him. And when Jesus saved the paralyzed man and later found him at the temple He said to him "See, you are well again. Stop sinning or something worse may happen to you." The only way to beat temptation and sin is by the word of God. God is stronger than any force anywhere within the universe. No matter what your battle is God can win it for you and allow you to repent. No matter how violent the storm is God commands nature and can save you from any storm you're in at any time.

I am very grateful to bring the Second Edition of "What Matters" to you. I attribute my strong faith to my family, my parents Leon and Mary Noorigian who brought me to St. Leon's Armenian Church every Sunday. My grandparents, Victoria and Mihran Noorigian both came from Armenia and it was an Apostolic faith. The Armenians were the first to join the Christian Crusaders because of their great faith. They were persecuted and killed for that faith but died reciting the Lord's Prayer in Armenian. That great faith is a part of me making me who I am. My sister, Marion Marti and my brother Aram Noorigian both played huge parts in my life. My mom's parents Rozard and Molly Polizzotti were the most loving grandparents you could hope for and they both helped to make me who I am. I thank my family deeply for their love and encouragement. My Mom is my best marketer for "What Matters" along with her Aunt Jenny Del'Aria. They are always handing my books out and buying more.

My father and mother-in-law, Harry and Helen Butler were very instrumental in my spiritual growth. They were Irish Catholic and the Catholic Church gave new meaning to Sunday mass for me. The Armenian mass was completely in Armenian but it was a three hour mass and when you left the church you knew you had been to church. The Catholic mass spoken entirely in English was much shorter but it explained everything that was happening during the mass. My mother-in-law was another dedicated Bible reader and she would subscribe me to daily scripture magazines and she got me into the daily Bible reading which I have come to look forward to every day. My father-in-law treated me as if I were his own. I thank my eight sisters and brothers-in-law, Elaine McCarthy, Anne Marlborough, Michael Butler, Tim Butler, Mary Jo Butler, Dorothy Fendt-Hanley, Kathy Butler aka Shraddah and Chris Butler, for being who they are and for encouraging me to be who I am.

I still need to thank my friends Kathy Wallace and Mary Ann Johnson for their continual encouragement to "do something with my poems". They always inspired me to write more poetry. They are both a big part of this book. And of course Brooke and all that comes with Brooke. I am forever grateful for Brooke and all that she brings to my life. I love that she gets that God loves her and that He's always going to love her. She would ask me "Mom does everything have to be a life lesson" and I would tell her Yes, that every opportunity I had to teach her something was very important and now I watch her share those lessons with her friends, she gives great sound advice.

And above all I thank God who makes all things possible. We have incredible power through Jesus Christ that we just need to tap into. Jesus promised that we could do great things with faith. I love the Apostle Peter which is where "Song To Peter" comes from. He loved Jesus with his whole heart and believed without question that He was the Son of God. Because of this faith he was able to walk on the water with Jesus until fear consumed him along with logic and both of those things told him he could not possibly walk on water and he sank. The Bible says he was immediately on the boat after he yelled "Save me Jesus", it doesn't say he swam to the boat or he had any trouble getting into the boat. Jesus immediately took him out of danger and placed him back into the boat. Those three words "Save me Jesus" can bring you out of the darkest places in an instant. And the power the Apostles were given by Jesus made them able to save people and heal them; simply by walking in Peter's shadow they were healed. Peter was just a man, a fisherman, when Jesus met him no different than you or me.

There is nothing more important than our relationship with God. Jesus promised He would return and on that great and terrible day we will need to know exactly what Jesus sounds like so we're not fooled by those trying until the very end to break us away from God. It will be a terrible day for those who do not know Him and a great day for those who know themselves and to whom they belong. Like any relationship it takes communication. I hope this book opens the communication between you and God. He is always there, always waiting for us to reach out to Him. He wants nothing more than to give us a good life, life in abundance. Take that good life with faith and courage and may God Bless You!

# Contents

# Your Love

Come let me feel the warmth of your true love beside me.
From all evil and wickedness and sickness please hide me.
Along the path to your kingdom I pray you will guide me.
I was once bound by Satan but your love has untied me.

My faith in your love, I believe is what saved me,
And the more my faith grew the more Satan craved me.
With every victory over temptation
my heart aches to praise thee.
Still with all I've been shown
your love will always amaze me.

Come let me feel your love that you give so freely.
By the power of your love you were able to free me.
God make me good in your eyes
so that my eyes may see thee
In your kingdom with your true love for all of eternity.

# A King

The spirit of God was upon Him,
Through Him prophesy was fulfilled,
God worked with Him and through Him,
And He did only as His father willed.

The miracles He performed made it clear,
And the people knew He was their king.
Those who ruled were filled with fear,
They knew their ruin He would bring.

He taught the people with love and mercy,
And revealed to them His father's love.
He told them what He was here to be,
That His Kingdom was from above.

Those in power He let take Him down,
He knew for this reason He was called.
With thorns they gave a king His crown,
To His own cross and death Jesus crawled.

God sent His Son to take our place,
To endure the penalty of our sin.
He knew the agony He would face,
To bring His people back to Him.

God shook the earth when Jesus died,
The holy temple trembled with fear.
"He was the Son of God" the people cried.
To those who killed Him it was clear.

For our salvation He suffered and bled,
His precious blood wipes away our stains.
He rose from death to glory just as He said
And now a king in Heaven He forever reigns.

# What Matters

How could she just sit there with everything going on?
By the time I take care of everything He will be gone.
I have to prepare a meal and serve the guests in my home,
And there she sits leaving me to do everything alone.

I have so many things to worry about
and she doesn't care.
She's anointing His feet and wiping them with her hair.
And He says, *"Martha, why do you*
*worry about meaningless things?*
*Your sister has chosen to do what matters*
*for the joy that it brings."*

And when He came back after my brother Lazarus had died
I told Him He could have come back
sooner and saved him if He tried.
And he said, *"Your brother shall rise;*
*I will bring him forth today,*
*I am the life and resurrection and*
*whoever believes will be saved"*.

Jesus went to the tomb and asked that
they clear away the stone,
And He spoke to His Father to show
He didn't do this alone.
And He thanked God for hearing
Him and called Lazarus' name.
And from the tomb, though dead for
days, my brother lived again.

There was no question but that He was
the Christ sent from above,
To show us there is no need to worry
if we trust in God's love.
And I learned it doesn't matter how
the rest of the world sees us;
All that matters is the time you spend at the feet of Jesus.

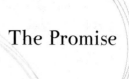

# The Promise

And suddenly right before my eyes after all of the pain,
My heart still breaking knowing it
would never be the same.
My tears still stinging, my tears falling like rain,
There He stood, larger than life, I had Him back again.

I listened to all His stories, I loved
listening to Him speak.
He made me feel I could do anything,
without Him I was weak.
I wanted to embrace Him, never let Him out of my sight,
I knew that with Him beside me
I'd never have to fear the night.

How can I explain the joy of having Him back again?
My spirit was lifted, my broken heart,
my heart began to mend.
I never thought I'd ever again lay eyes upon my friend,
After knowing how He had suffered
right to the bitter end.

And then He made a promise,
He said "I will always be near,
Though your eyes may not see me
you have nothing to fear,
And when the weight on your shoulders
seems too much to bear,
Call my name, believe this promise,
your voice I will hear".

# I Wish...

I wish I could have known you when
you walked upon this earth.
I wish I could have been there to
praise your blessed birth.
I wish I could have been with you
when you were just a boy,
Kissed by God, His beloved Son, filled with heavenly joy.

I wish I could have been there when
you fed your hungry lambs,
With holy bread and holy fish granted at your command.
I wish I could have been there when
you calmed the mighty sea
And ruled all of nature with such grand authority.

I wish I could have watched you as
you overpowered death,
And filled the lungs of Lazurus with
your own eternal breath.

I wish I could have seen you heal the
blind, the deaf, the lame,
And watched them leap and sing with
joy and praise your blessed name.

I wish I could have seen your glory
as you rose from the dead,
And moved the stone and left your
tomb to rise and live instead.
I wish I could have heard your angels
and had the courage to sing.
Yes, I will praise your name forever, Lord!
Blessed be Our King!

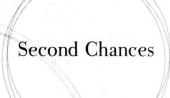

# Second Chances

Where would any of us be without second chances
And a hundred second chances after that?
We all start at the gate with the whole world before us
And sometimes we don't all make it back.

It's the second chance that will bring you home
No matter how many times you get off track.
God's love for you is strong. You will never be alone;
Your second chance will always bring you back.

# Tough People Do

When it's all over you remember tough times don't last.
Even in the eye of the storm remember this too shall pass.
And no matter what this time may
be putting you through
Never forget that tough times don't last, tough people do!

When the storm seems stronger
than what you can endure
And it feels never ending like you can't take anymore
Face the storm you're in with the
strength of God at your side
With His strength and your faith you will turn any tide.

No matter how violent the storm God is stronger still
And when the next storm rages as you know it will
Remember that tough times don't last, tough people do
And fear not for God will get you through this one too.

# Prayer

No matter how many times I see it
No matter how many times I'm shown
The power of prayer is greater
Than any other I have ever known.

"Ask and you shall receive"
Seems too simple to be true.
Still, no matter what I ask for
There's nothing He can't do.

Faith is all it takes.
Pray with faith and it's yours.
When there seems no way out
He will open all the doors.

Believe in what you ask for;
Ask it in His name.
Once you see what happens
Your life will never be the same.

Prayer is the key to life.
Life without prayer leaves you cold.
Unite your life with God.
Allow His love to make you bold.

He has always been here,
And He is always the same.
He is eager to grant you
What you ask for in His name.

No matter how many times
You get an answer to your prayers,
It will continue to astonish you
When you see how much He cares.

Pray every day with faith and love.
There's nothing God can't do.
It's a very precious thing to Him,
A prayer filled with faith from you.

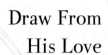

# Draw From
# His Love

He in heaven who made us loves us as only He can
With a depth of love no mortal mind
could truly understand.
But a love which was in existence before time began
Is what we need to draw from today
as we strive to live His command.

He in heaven who loves us is with us
through all of our days.
Even as we fall into temptation,
our Savior in heaven prays
That we will draw from His love
and seek His mercy that saves.
We just need to call on His name,
love Him and honor Him with praise.

He in heaven loves us no matter
where we might have been.
It's never too late to draw from
His love and start over again.
We must have faith in His forgiveness
and forgive all other men
And truly believe His love will heal us
and free us from sin.

His mercy can open any lock
but we must walk through the door,
Confess our sin, and allow Him to cleanse us
and make our hearts pure.
We just need to call on His name and
our place in heaven is assured
As long as we learn to obey Him and love Him
and know that Jesus is Lord.

# Get Up And Walk

Pick up your mat and walk!
Don't just talk the talk.
No matter where you are right now,
Pick up your mat and walk somehow.

The power is within you,
Incredible things you can do.
You're never too low don't ever let go,
Get off your mat and let the healing flow.

Stand up and let your faith heal you.
Let all those around feel you.
The grace that has brought you to your feet
Will be felt in some way by everyone you meet.

You have lives to change by your own story.
You were born to live boldly for His glory.
God's healing mercy will lift you to your feet;
He will lift you to victory in the midst of defeat.

Pick up your mat and walk!
Stop complaining it's only talk.
Do something instead inside your own head,
Forgive yourself even if you've made your own bed.

You have the power that God gave to you
To do all the things you need to do
You are forgiven but you need to move on
And take those chances before they're all gone!

# End Your Search

When the road you're walking on
feels like an uphill climb
And the load you're made to carry
gets heavier all the time,
You search for the solution that will
help support the weight.
The more questions you think you
answer the more you create.

You may search for your entire life and never find relief
From the load you're made to carry bringing only grief.
The world is full of people who will promise you a cure
If you only invest in their ideas,
they promise to sell you more.

It won't be long before new burdens
are added to the weight
And the promises made by people
no longer seem that great.
And you begin to believe this hardship
has somehow become your fate.
You stop searching for the solution
as you're certain it's too late.

Other people cannot help you;
they're not equipped for the role.
They're just as lost as you are on their
journey toward their goal.
There's only one source available that
will truly make you whole;
The answers you've been searching
for are deep within your soul.

Think about giving Jesus a chance to
fulfill the promises He made.
He promised He would hear you and
answer every time you prayed.
He already knows your needs and loves
you even if you've strayed.
Your soul is longing to unite with God
whose love will never fade.

Jesus promised He'd take our burdens,
our grief, and our pain.
He promised he would give us what
we asked for in His Name.
He promised that with faith our lives
would never be the same.
End your search with Jesus
let Him help you with your strain.
End your search with Jesus you have everything to gain.

# The Door

Stop long enough until you can hear it and then listen
To the voice deep inside that you so often ignore.
It's there to help you to make the right choices
And take you higher than you've ever been before.

Just be still and listen, and let the voice take you
To that higher place, and don't be afraid to soar.
It's all about living and growing and learning
To recognize the voice that will let you be sure.

Stay tuned to that voice, and know when it speaks;
It will tenderly nudge you or it will wage a war.
It will battle the will of your weak human spirit.
Don't question where it will lead; dare to explore.

It will lead you to places you've never dreamed of before
Like the kingdom of heaven that's just through the Door.
Follow the voice of the Lord; He's what you're longing for.
Through the Door you will find your
treasure and search no more.

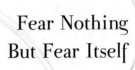

# Fear Nothing
# But Fear Itself

God asked me to stand up for righteousness sake.
He said I have laid kings and princes at your feet.
He said the good land is here, yours to take
I will help you through any obstacles you meet.

I did this and He was bringing me to the good land.
Encouraged was I to face my enemy and win.
God was watching over me I was in the Lord's hand.
He said stand up for me and show the enemy their sin.

I was to take that land with faith and bravery.
God laid the land before me and said this is yours.
He gave me the courage to be all I had to be
And He was bringing me safely to the shore.

Without warning I allowed fear to enter my heart.
Satan was standing up for the wicked against me.
My faith was shaken, the devil would not depart.
I no longer had the courage to be what I had to be.

Fear would not allow me to enter the good land.
God was handing it to me but fear got in the way.
I was not able to follow through as God had planned.
And the good land that was offered me was taken away.

# Day After Day

"Just let me go back for a minute", the rich man said,
"So that I can warn my family of what lies ahead.
I'm sure they'd do things differently if they only knew
That you're paid back for everything
you did and didn't do.

"I would have cared for Lazarus who
begged outside my door.
He was always there, a nuisance, he became an eye sore.
Day after day he'd lie outside my
beautiful mansion pleading,
And day after day I'd walk right by ignoring his needing.

"I had wonderful garments, I had riches beyond compare,
And now I find myself in this awful place I just can't bear.
Lazarus had nothing, no clothes, no pride, no charms.
And now I see him day after day
cradled in Abraham's arms.

"He who possessed nothing is now in
the presence of God above.
His wounds are healed, he's fed,
he no longer hungers for love.
And I had everything, the best;
I wouldn't settle for any less,
And now I'm naked, cold, and all alone in this wilderness.

"Just let me go back to warn the rest
of my family of what's to be.
I could save them from this place
if they could just see me."
But he was told that he was told so
many times in many ways
That the compassion you show others
comes back to you one day.

So care for those you meet, greet
everyone with love and respect.
You may not think it makes a difference
but it has a huge effect
On where you will spend your time
when you are no longer here.
Humble yourself, lose your pride, and
the rest will become clear.

# Standing Strong
## With God

Have great faith in the Lord your God
and all He has in store for you.
His love is like that of a loving father
there's nothing He wouldn't do.
For those He has chosen to call His
own, He can make you like new.
And with His love and His strength
there's nothing you can't do.

Live in this truth and believe it is true
every day with all your heart
And the blessings you receive from
God will be way off the chart.
There's nothing in this world that
could tear you and God apart.
The power He has given you has been
yours right from the start.

God has given you power to stand strong
against any evil force before you.
He has given you authority to overcome
the enemy in everything you do.
And He will give you the courage you need
when you fight for what is true.
Stand firm in that faith knowing that
this power is given to you.

Do not be afraid for God will always
provide to those who believe it is so,
Even as you face your trials you can face
them with trust and always know
That God will bring you through and
through it your faith will grow
And you can remain strong without fear
knowing God will never let you go.

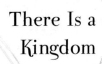

# There Is a
# Kingdom

More magnificent than the golden red of a sunset in July
More brilliant than the crystal blue of a clear autumn sky
More intense than the blaze of the
constant rays of the sun
The place from where time began
can be compared to none.

The eyes we've been given have
beheld nothing quite like this.
If you never experience pure perfection,
it will never be missed.
The golden reds of a sunset and the
bright blue hue of the sky
Will produce a sense of satisfaction,
of perfection to your eye.

There is a Kingdom that exists with
no limits of time or space.
Its magnificence cannot be explained,
interpreted, or erased.
There is a Kingdom where you can
look upon God's holy face
Where you can hear the voice of an
angel, there is such a place.

More love than the most caring
mother could have ever shown.
More kindness, peace, and harmony
than you or I have ever known.
More comfort and compassion where
you will never feel alone.
There is a Kingdom that waits for
those who God calls His own.

# Take Time
# to Praise

Give praise to the Father in everything you do.
His power is all-consuming; His unending love is true.
He deserves your praise; He makes everything new.
He battles evil every moment; He's fighting for you.

Give praise to the Father before beginning your day;
Before your troubles take over, make time to pray.
He's waiting for you; it doesn't matter what you say;
The words will come to you; praise Him today.

Give praise to the Son; He deserves it as well.
He left the world He knew to save those who fell.
He called those who would listen; He had stories to tell
Of the kingdom of heaven and a place called hell.

All those that would listen were saved by His grace.
He's still saving the souls of those in His embrace.
He longs to save you. Don't lose sight of His face
And He will give you the strength to finish the race.

Give praise to the Holy Spirit of God up above
Who gave praise to the Son in the form of a dove;
With the Father and Son He forms the trinity of love.
He's the comforter the Spirit of God Jesus spoke of.

Take time to speak to the Spirit, the Father, and the Son.
Cherish the knowledge that they
love you as no other one.
They long to feel your love before your time here is done.
Give thanks and praise and your victory will be won.

# The Edge

There he sits on the edge of his bed
with a gun to his head
Wondering if he'd be better off dead.
The dread is overtaking him; he tries so hard to find
Something good in his life, wishing
he could stop the rewind.

There is nothing left but hopelessness and regret.
He is too close to the edge; his soul is too far in debt.
He stares into space. The only color he sees is gray.
His world is black and white. He can't face another day.

How did this happen to him? Where did he go wrong?
He was on top of the world looking lean and strong.
But the world was on top of him;
he was under the weight
Of regret for the things that have
brought him to this fate.

There he sits on the edge of his bed
with a gun to his head
Wondering where those other paths might have lead.
Now his soul is a wasteland; empty except for hate
For himself and his actions and he's sure it's too late.

He drops the gun to the floor and
holds his head and cries
For all the heartbreak he has caused, and again he tries
To remember the reason why he should live another day
But he can't find one; it's so painful watching the replay.

Even in this hour, God the Father watches from above,
Praying that he remembers the only reason is love.
Not that he loves God but that God loved him
Enough to go out on a limb to take away his sin.

And God loves him even as he sits on the edge of his bed.
Like a loving father, He longs to take away all the dread.
His debt has been paid; his soul is free from sin.
God prays now that His child will call on Him.

# May's Glory

It happens in an instant; in an instant a life can change,
And all the things you know somehow become strange.
Those things that were so important just the day before
Become nothing in that instant;
they don't matter anymore.

We watched you with such admiration, love, and fear.
As you walked through that door you left us all here.
And we prayed and we loved you
and we prayed some more
That you'd come back to us and be stronger than before.

With every step you had to take
we were there at your side
Keeping you strong in our love, a love we cannot hide.
We sent our cards and our meals
that were made with care.
Even though you couldn't see us we
were somehow always there.

And then our prayers were answered
and you came back home
To the people who love you like you were their very own.
It's a family we've created and it's rare today, we're told,
But all we cared about was that you
came back to the fold.

Your family and friends thought of
all the reasons they cared.
They brought to mind all the wonderful
things they've shared
With someone who means so much in so many ways.
You will remain a part of us all for the rest of our days.

# God So Loved The World

God so loved the world
That He sent His only Son.
He suffered and died for our sin
And our victory was won.

God so loved the world
He raised His Son from the dead
So we might have life through Him
By the innocent blood He shed.

God so loved the world
Even though it was depraved.
Those who love His Son
Are the ones who will be saved.

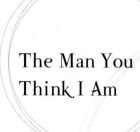

# The Man You Think I Am

He said I wish I could be the man that you think I am.
My confidence says I can't but you believe I can.
I know that I am not half the man you had in your plan,
When you formed me out of nothing and my life began.

He says I want to be what you have created me to be.
I want to walk in your light and do what is right,
Know how to reject evil when it tries to tempt me
And be strengthened by your love, power and might.

I want to not be affected by the world and its ways;
It promises you happiness then it takes it away.
You are always there through even my darkest days.
Your promises are real I know that each time I pray.

I want to look in the mirror and see the man that you see;
The one who has been set free to be all that I can be.
I want to do all those things you have planned for me,
Resist evil, remain free, live my life more abundantly.

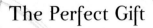

# The Perfect Gift

I've read the laws as received by Moses
And learned the penalty that sin imposes.
For sinners, the door to God always closes
And we all fall short according to Moses.

Salvation appeared impossible for anyone,
With God's laws, it seemed it couldn't be done.
Salvation was lost when time had first begun
When Adam and Eve put their trust in the evil one.

There is no hope for us in this world on our own.
And with no hope of salvation we can never atone,
But there's wonderful news: we're no longer alone.
God sent His Son to love us and bring us back home.

We've done nothing to deserve salvation, even to this day.
It's a priceless gift from our Father we could never repay.
The only blameless one died in order to show us the way.
His blood paid for our sins; remember that when you pray.

Recall the laws God set in place thousands of years ago.
Obey those laws with all your might
and let everybody know
That salvation is possible if you believe
in Jesus and never let go
Of the promise he made of eternal life
For those who believe it is so.

# Song to Peter

Empty nets were all you had to show after
being on Lake Gennesaret all night.
You struggle to bring your boat to shore when
something peculiar catches your sight.
It's a man speaking to thousands of people
who are clinging to His every word.
They push Him to the water's edge.
He boards your boat, and your heart is stirred.

After His sermon, He asked that you pull
your boat out and cast your nets again.
You tell Him there were no fish all night.
He promised He'd make you a fisher of men.
You drop your nets, and as soon as you do,
they are tearing from the strain.
You filled two boats with the fish you caught,
and you never looked back again.

It was you who walked on the water with Him.
What a miraculous thing to do.
You doubted; you sank and cried,
"Save me, Jesus," and you were the first who knew.
When asked what people say of Him, it was you
who confessed He was the Son of Man.
He blessed you, Simon, and named you Peter,
the rock, on whom His church would stand.

Salt of the earth, light of the world, you were
sent among wolves to preach His word.
You showed them signs they'd never seen,
taught them things they'd never heard.
How you begged Him not to return to
Jerusalem where he told you He would die
And it was you who saw Him being lead away
and all three times you would deny.

Oh, Peter, how your heart must have ached for
having denied knowing the King of kings,
But he knew you were grieving. He knew how
you loved Him; He knew all these things.
And how your heart must have been lifted up
when you visited the tomb of the Son of Man
And found an angel where the Lord had been
who told you of the fulfillment of God's plan.

Never again would your nets be empty;
you filled them with believers again and again.
The very Spirit of Jesus was within your soul
as you preached His victory over sin.
Faith provided strength to fight the good fight
and you fought for Christ to the end.
You devoted your life to the Lord and His people
and you truly became God's fisher of men.

# Times Like These

It's times like these when I'm so at ease.
Everything's right, and life's a breeze.
That's when I stop and get on my knees
And say thank you Jesus for times like these.

You make these times that are so right.
Life's a joy and the future's bright.
That's when I pray with all my might
That you'll always keep me in your sight.

And I pray that you'll hear me when I say
I love you, Jesus, bless your children today.
It's times like these when it's going my way
That I thank you Jesus all night and day.

# Overcoming Evil

The devil is far worse than the worst
person you will ever know.
Worse than the worst thing you could
imagine, he can make it so.
His role in the world is to keep you
away from God and His ways
He uses every chance to turn you
away from God every day.

No matter how good a person you
are he will always be there.
He will stop you from reaching your
goal by using your fear.
He will distort your vision until your
path is no longer clear.
And regardless of the path you take
evil will always be there.

The devil has free reign in this world
but God is still in control.
Even when you fall you can call Him
and He can save your soul.
Draw near to God and He will stay
with you and keep you whole.
Overcoming evil with faith in God
should always be our goal.

# The Seeds of Life

And His word became seed
planted in the heart of man.
On the path they hear the word
But they do not understand;
So evil takes the seed leaving them
With less than when they began.

Some of the seed fell on rocky ground
And although they gladly accept the word
The rock wouldn't allow the seed to grow,
So even though their hearts were stirred
When trouble and persecution come
They fall away rejecting what they heard.

Some hear the message loud and clear
And they put their hope in the message they hear
And the seed takes root and begins to grow
But the thorn bushes around them choke them with fear

And all their worries and their love for money
Stop them from bearing fruit when the harvest is so near.

It is in the good soil that they hear the word
And the seed is planted and they understand it well.
The soil is deep and so the roots are strong
And within the word those in the good soil dwell.
They bear good fruit a hundred times over
And so others receive the message by the stories they tell.

# It's You

It's you who made the sky so blue
And filled it with stars at night.
Before any colors, before any light;
Before anything there was you.
And you made the sky so blue.

It's you who made the trees so tall
And covered them with leaves of green.
Before any plants or colors were seen;
It was you before anything at all.
And you made the trees so tall.

It's you who made the sea so deep
And filled it with life overflowing.
Before any water could start anything growing,
Before anyone could begin to reap,
It was you who made the fish in the sea so deep.

It's you who made the mountains so high
Reaching up to the stars in your brilliant sky.
Before anyone could attempt to wonder why,
Before anyone could live or die,
It was you who made the mountains high.

It's you who made the sun so bright
To warm the planet earth down below
Before anyone could begin to know.
It was you before there was any dark or light.
It was you before there was day or night.

It's you who made heaven and called it your home
And filled it with angels to ever sing your praise.
Before any song, before any voice could be raised,
It was you, Father, in heaven sitting upon your thrown.
It's still you, Almighty Father, still calling us home.

# Our Father's Voice

Quietly we wait and hope to hear our Father's voice.
To learn His will and obey; it's us
who've made that choice.
God only wants what's good for us;
He knows all of our needs.
So we are waiting to hear His word
and follow where it leads.

Prayerfully we wait for God to speak into our hearts.
Our faith grows stronger every day once the healing starts
Until we find ourselves listening for His voice constantly
And trusting that His word alone is what will set us free.

With open hearts, we invite the Holy Spirit of the one
Whom God has sent to be our friend,
His own begotten Son.
He gives to us His mercy and He frees us from our sin.
And the Holy Spirit within our
hearts brings us home again.

Life we've learned is better when
we seek God's Kingdom first
And drink from the living water
that will satisfy our thirst.
It is His will we ask be done;
it's us who've made that choice.
So we ask in the name of Jesus,
let us hear Our Father's voice.

# Seven More

Looking back he finds it amazing how
all these things played out,
And the difficult lesson to be learned
was learned without a doubt.
It all began with a single thought until
the thought took control,
And with every thought he found
himself falling deeper in a hole.

Every single action you take first begins
with a thought inside your head,
And whether that thought is good or
bad you're already being lead.
He knew about the love of God and
the direction he should take
But temptation was there every day
until he felt that he might break.

The enticement was there for the taking,
    the attraction was so strong.
His world was black and white, no gray,
    and he knew right from wrong.
With everything he had he fought
until the thought was finally gone,
And with a sense of relief he felt he was
    free and started to move on.

It was then that he heard the voices,
    they were screaming inside his head
What he thought he had overcome
    had become his biggest dread.
The temptation was different this time,
    it was stronger than before
The evil thought he fought had left
    but returned with seven more.

He found himself in a place he hated
    and only sadness was his friend.
He was bound by Satan who brought other
    demons to bring him to his end.
They allowed no thoughts that could lift
    him only his suffering was for real.
They pulled him further away from God,
    His love and mercy he couldn't feel.

It took everything he had to find the truth,
he knew the truth would set him free.
Somehow he found himself back in God's
grace, nowhere else he'd rather be.
Through the pain he learned that when
temptation enters as it always will,
Stay strong in the spirit knowing that you
will need to become stronger still.

Evil will return when you cast him out
and bring with him seven more.
The strength of this war against your
spirit is greater than the one before.
Call upon the angels of God to minister
to you and to strengthen your soul.
They will bring your prayers to God who
will rescue you and make you whole.

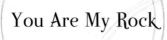

# You Are My Rock

You are the rock that I'm anchored to.
You watch and see everything I go through.
You know my love for you is strong and true,
Despite some of the things I say and do.

You love me still, though I'm weak and frail.
Even when I'm tested and clearly fail.
When holding my breath, you help me exhale,
Get me back on my feet, and you help me prevail.

You are my rock, my strength on which I rely.
You open my wings while you teach me to fly.
Don't let me go; I'm getting closer to the sky.
Hold my wings open, Lord. I truly want to try.

You are my rock, my truth, and my light.
I want to fly with you with all of my might.
Please, Lord, don't let me out of your sight.
Stay with me, and I will surely win this fight.

# Imagine John

Imagine for a moment, if you could.
Imagine. Humor me, if you would.
Imagine you're the closest one to the Lord.
Of all His apostles, you're the most adored.

Imagine, if you will, that you were at His side
When He turned water to wine for
the groom and his bride
And all those at the wedding feast
remarked that this wine
Was the finest of spirits to ever come from a vine.

Imagine that you're John, the beloved apostle, the one
Who witnessed many miracles once they had begun.
Imagine you are with Him while He prays to God above;
A Son speaking to His Father with reverence and love.

Imagine being with the Lord day in and day out,
And learning firsthand what God's love is about.
And walking with Jesus sharing many special things.
Imagine being His favorite and the joy that this brings.

Imagine never leaving Him even when He faced His death.
Imagine Him speaking to you with His last dying breath.
Imagine the Book of Revelation being shown just to you.
Imagine sweet John and all the heavenly things He knew.

Imagine just for a moment, if you would dare to try,
Knowing that you'll be with Jesus on the very day you die.
Imagine you are the closest to being perfect in His eye.
Imagine John, the beloved apostle,
on whom God could rely.

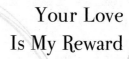

# Your Love
# Is My Reward

You fill my heart with joy and make that joy complete.
You help me to see the good in everyone I meet.
You help me find my prize even in defeat,
And you let me find the truth in the midst of deceit.

This world would like to hide you and all you represent.
Your followers hear your words and
know what you meant
When you spoke of sin and our ability to repent.
We know you and the Father and
the reason you were sent.

The truth sustains me and helps me stay on course.
The evil one tempts me while feeling no remorse.
But I have you and your love to fight any evil force.
I draw from that power, and Jesus you're the source.

You fill my heart with joy and lead me every day.
Closer to your own heart which is where I long to stay.
I know your words and know those
words will never betray
The faith I have in you, Lord, and
the price you had to pay.

My heart is filled with gladness because you are my Lord.
You help me in my fight for life;
you are my shield and sword.
Only goodness surrounds me. My salvation is assured.
As long as I keep you in my heart your love is my reward.

# The King's Feast

The invites were sent by the king a long
time ago at last the feast was set.
There was gold, fine linens, the choicest
foods, his son deserved the best.
He sent his servants to bring the guests
to the long awaited wedding fest.
But instead they mistreated some of his
servants and others killed the rest.

The king became enraged and sent his
troops, his wrath had been renown.
He ordered them to be destroyed and
he burned their city down.
They were undeserving to attend the feast
and so the king looked around
And asked his servants to go out again
and invite everyone they found.

There were good and bad alike, the palace
was completely filled with guests.
They were eating and drinking for the first
time in their lives they had all the best.
When the king saw a certain man he asked
how he had gotten in with the rest
The man was silent, he could not stay
because of the way that he was dressed.

The king ordered he be bound by his hands
and feet and thrown into the night
To suffer and cry and gnash his teeth because
his repentant heart was not right.
And He said the Kingdom of God is much
like this and it is right before your sight.
Make straight your path make pure your
heart and remain within His light.

# Walk With You

Lost in my own head, thoughts scattered all about.
Remembering the things you said, not having a doubt
That you are here with me every step of the way.
Everything I do you see; you hear everything I say.

Everything that's said to me is clearly heard by you.
From these lies set me free to only hear what's true.
Help me see what's real as if looking through your eyes.
Help me only feel the things that let me grow inside.

You are with me always. Please don't put me down.
I see every one of my days as I look along the ground.
There you are; just as you said, I'm cradled in your hand.
Through this dread I only see your footprints in the sand.

I trust in you and your love for me and all that is true.
I know that you are here for me to help me follow through.
Give me the strength I need to walk with you side by side.
Keep me strong in thought and deed and always be my guide.

# Today

Open your eyes to a brand new day.
Let yesterday's troubles fade away.
Tomorrow is another whole day away.
Live in the wonder and splendor of today!

This is a gift, you see, another day.
A gift for you to do with as you may.
Disappointment will only waste it away.
Don't spend it reliving yesterday.

Wrap both arms around this brand new day.
Embrace the new opportunities on their way.
Don't let God's gift to you simply slip away.
Live every moment to the fullest today.

# Speak Into My Heart, Oh Lord

Speak into my heart, oh Lord,
Show me all your ways,
Protect me all my days,
Keep me in your gaze.

Speak into my heart, oh Lord,
Show me how to live,
Help me to forgive,
Forgive the things I did.

Speak into my heart, oh Lord,
Show me what to say,
Keep the evil one away,
Hear me when I pray.

Speak into my heart, oh Lord,
Show me all your ways,
Help me through this maze,
Stay with me always.

Speak into my heart, oh Lord,
I know that you're the one
Who made the moon and sun
And me and everyone.

Speak into my heart, oh Lord,
Show me what to do
To show others it is true
That we can rely on you.

Speak into my heart, oh Lord,
Let me work for you,
Show me what to do,
To show others it is true
That our only hope is you.

Thank you so much for reading the Second Edition of *What Matters*. I hope it has inspired you to begin a relationship or strengthen your relationship with God and His beloved Son, Jesus. There is no relationship in this world more important than the one we will have with God. That relationship will change everything in your world for the better. We must always remember that God loves us as if we were the only person in the world, the only person He has to look after. And we must never forget the power He has given us through His Son, Jesus Christ. We have been given power to accomplish great things in His name. Anyone you give this book to will be so appreciative that you did, it will help them through whatever they are going through when you give the book to them. It is a blessing to be able to see the reaction of those who have read it. It is a blessing to have shared this book with you.

To order additional copies please visit
https://www.tatepublishing.com/bookstore/
book.php?w=9781631850615.

To contact me directly for signed copies please
visit www.facebook.com/debra.butler.1257.
I would love to hear from you.

God bless each and every one of you. Live in the confident belief that you are loved and cared for by God every day. Thank you.